The Littlest Donut

By

Charley Randazzo

The littlest donut in all of the town,
her frosting was pink, and her sprinkles were brown.
Each morning she'd look in the mirror and say,
“I'll grow up to be a big donut one day!”

But one day she woke and was rather appalled.
Somehow it felt as if she had gone bald.
She reached to her head then she shuddered in fear.
Her sprinkles were gone they had just disappeared

This was a big problem - most people don't know,
that donuts need sprinkles for more than just show.
Sprinkles give power to one and to all,
so donuts need them to grow big, strong and tall.

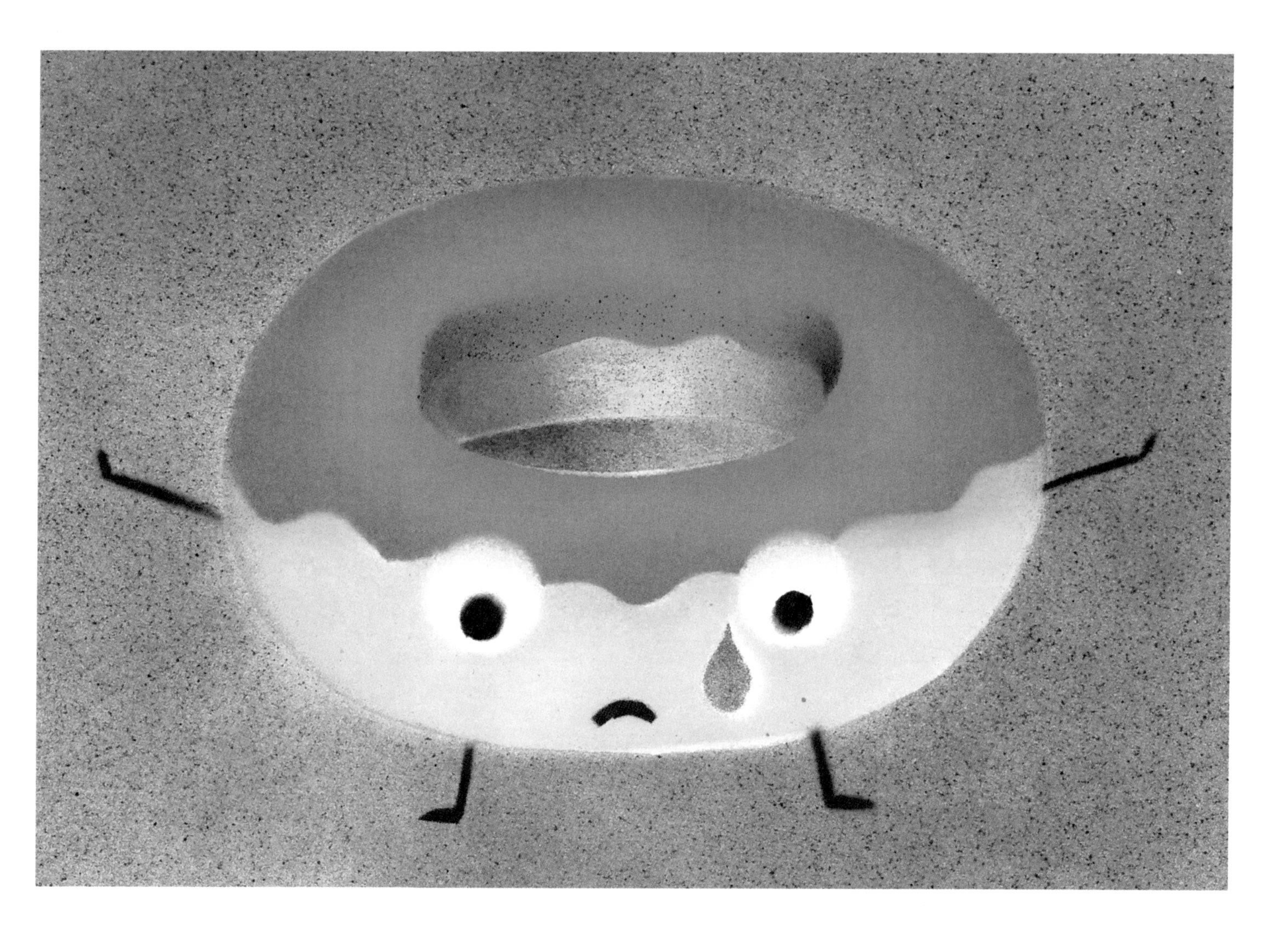

Now since she was little and wanted to grow,
she went to find sprinkles, she'd search high and low.
She knew she'd succeed but she'd have to be clever.
"I will NOT be the littlest donut forever!"

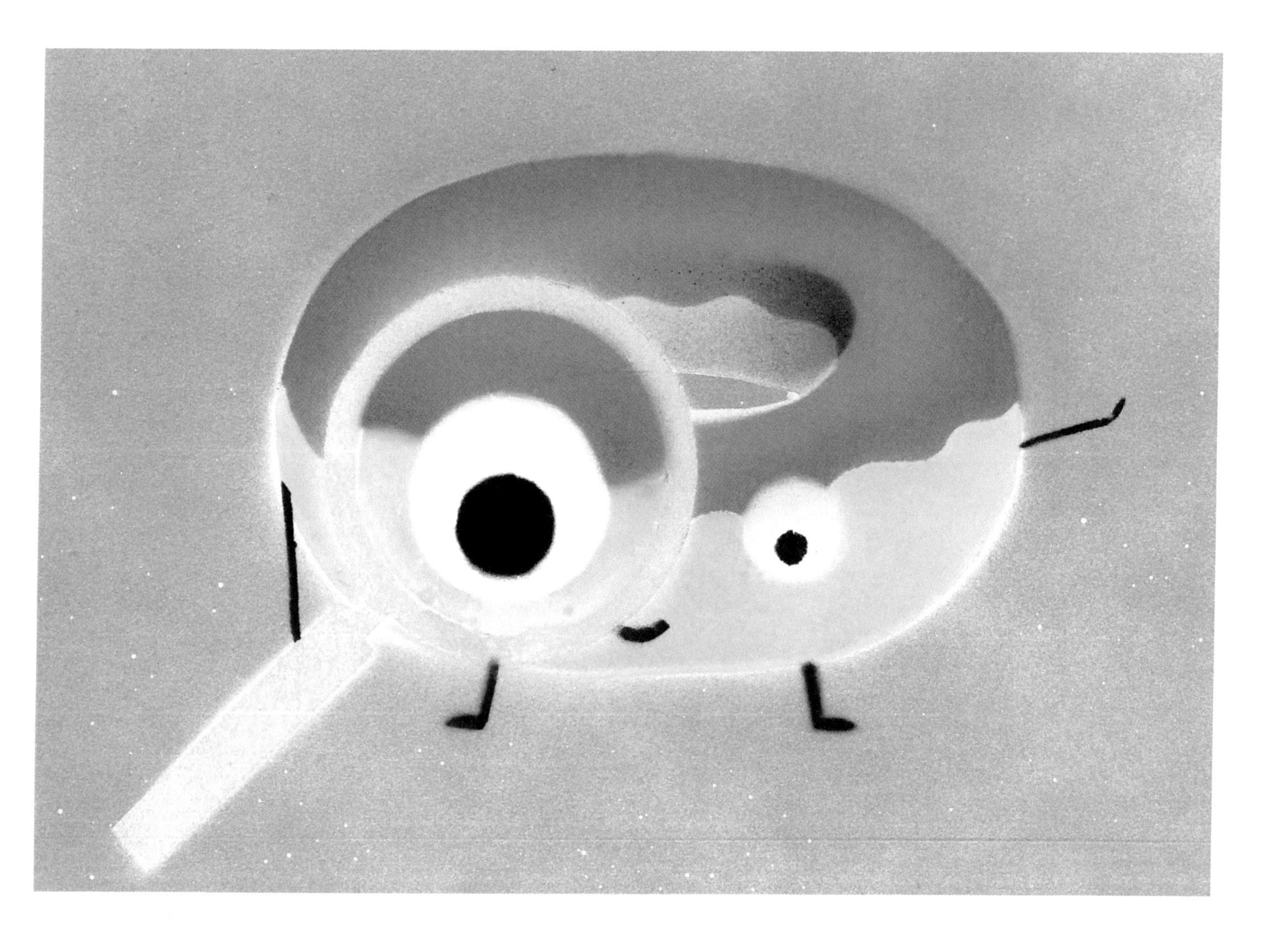

She found her best friend, a most loyal fellow,
a chocolate glazed donut whose sprinkles were yellow.
He listened to her as she told her sad tale,
and gave her a hug shouting "you will prevail"

Then he found a solution with utmost efficiency.
"I know how we'll fix your sprinkle deficiency!"
He reached up on top of his head and declared,
"You can have some of mine I have plenty to share"

The littlest donut felt grateful and blessed.
She thanked her best friend and set off on her quest.
With her chin up she skipped in the forward direction,
in search of more sprinkles to complete her collection.

Along came her neighbor, a sight to be seen,
a tall cone of ice cream whose sprinkles were green.
"I noticed you're missing some sprinkles" she said.
"So why don't you take some of mine instead?"

"Oh that would be lovely," the donut rejoiced.
She thanked her then said in a confident voice,
"With everyone helping me out in this way,
I'll have enough sprinkles by the end of the day."

News was now spreading far across the land,
and soon the whole town came to lend her a hand.
"I heard you need sprinkles – I want to help too,"
cried a red velvet cupcake whose sprinkles were blue.

Then a brownie, a cookie and a nice slice of cake
all offered their sprinkles for the donut to take.
Before it was time to get ready for bed,
she had a full rainbow on top of her head.

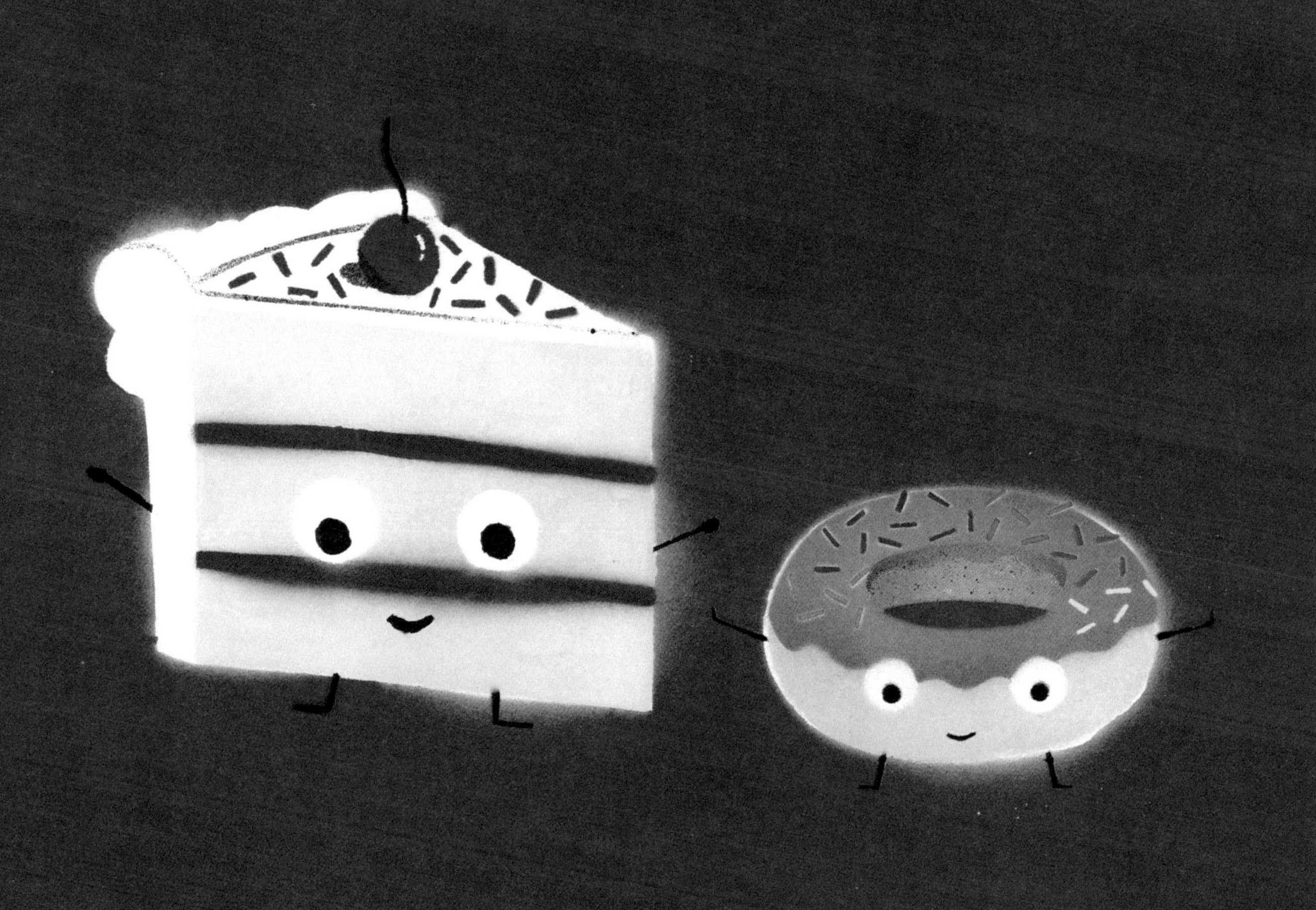

The donut grew older and after some years,
she became big and strong, despite what she once feared.
And as she was minding her business one day,
a littler donut came walking her way

"I see that you lost all your sprinkles lil' guy.
I know you feel sad, but there's no need to cry."
She plucked off a few of her own in a hurry
and handed them over shouting "don't you worry."

"I too lost my sprinkles a long time ago.
I didn't know what to do or where to go.
But I have no doubt that you'll quickly recover,
as long as you trust in the kindness of others."

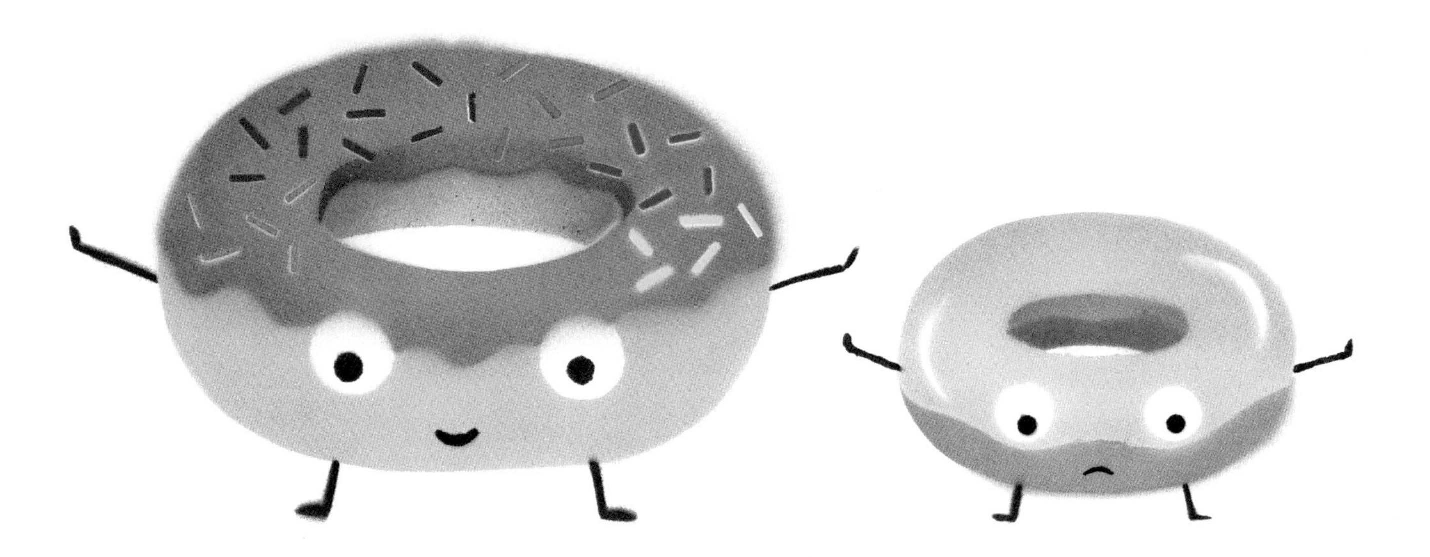

The littler donut could now understand
and accepted the sprinkles she placed in his hand.
He smiled knowing he wasn't in this alone
and left to make a rainbow all of his own.

THE END

Made in the USA
Coppell, TX
05 March 2023